P9-DNO-023

THE TIME WARP TRIO series

Knights of the Kitchen Table

The Not-So-Jolly Roger

The Good, the Bad, and the Goofy

Your Mother Was a Neanderthal

2095

Tut, Tut

Summer Reading Is Killing Me!

It's All Greek to Me

See You Later, Gladiator

Sam Samurai

Hey Kid, Want to Buy a Bridge?

Viking It and Liking It

Me Oh Maya

THE TIME WARP TRIO

Da Wild, Da Crazy, Da Vinci

by Jon Scieszka

illustrated by Adam McCauley

VIKING

VIKING
Published by Penguin Group
Penguin Young Readers Group, 345 Hudson Street, New York, New York 10014, U.S.A.
Penguin Group (Canada), 10 Alcorn Avenue, Toronto, Ontario, Canada M4V 3B2
(a division of Pearson Penguin Canada Inc.)
Penguin Books Ltd, 80 Strand, London WC2R 0RL, England
Penguin Ireland, 25 St Stephen's Green, Dublin 2, Ireland (a division of Penguin Books Ltd)
Penguin Group (Australia), 250 Camberwell Road, Camberwell, Victoria 3124, Australia
(a division of Pearson Australia Group Pty Ltd)
Penguin Books India Pvt Ltd, 11 Community Centre, Panchsheel Park, New Delhi - 110 017, India
Penguin Group (NZ), Cnr Airborne and Rosedale Roads, Albany,
Auckland, New Zealand (a division of Pearson New Zealand Ltd)
Penguin Books (South Africa) (Pty) Ltd, 24 Sturdee Avenue, Rosebank,
Johannesburg 2196, South Africa

Penguin Books Ltd, Registered Offices: 80 Strand, London WC2R 0RL, England

Published in 2004 by Viking, a division of Penguin Young Readers Group.

1 3 5 7 9 10 8 6 4 2

Illustrations by Adam McCauley

Library of Congress cataloging-in-publication data is available.
ISBN: 0-670-05926-9

Printed in U.S.A.
Set in Sabon

To a real Renaissance guy—Scott Sellers

J. S.

For Gardiner Dad Vinci

A. M.

ONE

"Ready! . . . Aim! . . . "

"Wait!" yelled Sam. He fixed his glasses to take a better look. "We're supposed to be in Italy."

Fred, Sam, and I were standing with our backs to a steep, sandy hill. It looked like it could be Italy. But there was a strange-looking invention sitting in front of us—a wooden, flying-saucer-shaped thing, about as big as an ice cream truck.

The size wasn't the scary part. The scary part was the guns sticking out of it. The even scarier part was knowing the word that usually comes after "Ready! Aim!"

"You're lucky we didn't end up in a giant toilet," said Fred. "But now you'd better figure out what to do about those guns pointed our way."

I looked at the wooden flying-saucer tank. Fred was right. Half of its guns were pointed right at us.

"Greetings, um, whoever you are in there," I said. "We are peaceful travelers, just looking around for a guy named Leonardo da Vinci. Ever heard of him?"

A man with a short, dark beard, who wore a reddish-colored robe, stepped out from behind a group of small trees.

"Who asks for Leonardo da Vinci?" said the man.

"We ask for Leonardo da Vinci," I said. "I mean me, I'm Joe. This is Fred. That's Sam."

The man stepped closer and looked us over. He was half smiling in a way that looked very familiar.

"This guy had better not be Thomas Crapper," said Fred.

"We're looking for Leonardo da Vinci because

we have this *Book,*" I said. "And we have a drawing in our *Book* just like one of the drawings from Leonardo's book."

Now the man looked surprised. "You have seen my notebooks?"

Sam figured it out in a second. "Your notebooks? Of course. We *are* in Italy. It is you. You're just younger than you were in that drawing we saw with the white hair and white beard."

Now the man looked very confused.

Sam kept babbling anyway. "I knew it. I knew it. I knew it. Leonardo da Vinci. Leonardo the scientist. Leonardo the inventor. You are Leonardo."

"Yes," said the man slowly. "I am Leonardo da Vinci. You know me. But I don't know you. You seem so young to be spies." Leonardo waved one hand. Two of Leonardo's men came out from behind his wooden tank invention, carrying a long piece of rope. They tied Fred, Sam, and me together.

"It's always the same thing," said Leonardo. "Someone trying to steal my ideas."

"Oh no," said Sam. "We are big fans of yours. We love your ideas. Your giant crossbow. Your cannons. Your submarine. . . ."

Now Leonardo looked shocked. "How do you know about these things?"

I saw Sam was getting us deeper in trouble. I spoke up before he could do any more damage. "Oh he's just guessing," I said. "We're not spies. We're inventors too. And we're not from anywhere near here. We're Joe, Sam, and Fred . . . da Brooklyn."

"I don't think I know that town," said Leonardo.

"No, I didn't think you would," I said. "But we came from there looking for a thin blue *Book* with strange writing and drawings and pictures so we can maybe ask you a few questions about how it works and then get right back to Brooklyn and never bother you again, really. Have you seen it around?"

"A notebook?"

said Leonardo. "Blue? With drawings and writing? Like this?"

Leonardo pulled out a thin blue notebook.

We were saved.

Birds tweeted in the trees. Water bubbled happily in the stream. It was a beautiful morning.

"So you do have *The Book*. You are the inventor of *The Book*," said Sam. "This is amazing. It's the first time we ever managed to time warp someplace we wanted to . . . *and* find *The Book* right away."

Even Fred was impressed. "Wow," he said. "And before we warp back home, Mr. Leonardo, I would just like to say you draw some pretty fine stuff."

"Absolutely," I said. "We liked all of your drawings. Even the ones of those strange looking people. Those were weird . . . but good."

"Leonardo da Vinci," said Sam. "Wow."

Leonardo stared at us. Something wasn't quite right.

"So if you could just have your guys come back and untie us," I said, "we'll just ask you a quick couple of questions about *The Book*. How it works and stuff like that. Then you can get back to testing your wooden tank thing."

"No one has seen my notebooks," said Leonardo. He put the small blue book back in his robe. "If you have seen them, you must be spies. And there is only one solution for spies." He stepped back and waved to his wooden tank. It wheeled around sideways so even more guns pointed at us.

"Oh no," said Sam. "This is worse than getting flushed down a giant toilet. Do something, Joe."

Fred struggled against the rope. "Stall them with a trick."

I tried to think of a trick. Any trick.

"Ready! . . . " said Leonardo.

All I could think of was that we had just met the great Leonardo da Vinci.

"Aim! . . ." said Leonardo.

All I could think of was that we were going to get blasted by an invention of the great Leonardo da Vinci.

"FI—"

OWT

Wait a minute. I can't let us end like that. Six pages into the story and the Time Warp Trio gets it? Without any explanation? That's not right.

I have to at least try to explain how three regular guys from Brooklyn found themselves face-to-face with Leonardo da Vinci, somewhere in Italy, somewhere around the year 1500.

It all happened because of inventions.

Well—it really all happened because of one invention.

You probably won't believe it when I tell you this invention isn't a rocket, or any kind of machine at all. It's a book called . . . *The Book*.

I know this doesn't sound like much of an invention. But *The Book* is not like any other book. It's a book that warps time and space. I got it as a birthday present from my uncle Joe. He's a magician. Not a very good one.

The Book is one amazing invention. It has taken Fred, Sam, and me one hundred years into the future and thousands of years into the past. We sailed with Vikings in 1000. We fought Japanese samurai warriors in 1600. We saw the Brooklyn Bridge getting built in 1877. And that was just in the last few months.

The not-so-amazing part of this invention is that we don't really know how *The Book* works. Sometimes a picture sets it off. Sometimes it's words. One time a magic square of numbers got it started. All we know is that when *The Book* starts leaking its pale green time-traveling mist, it takes us to some other time and place.

No time passes at home while we are gone. The only way to get back home is to find *The Book*. And we always seem to get in trouble no matter where we go.

So like I was saying, this time warp is all about inventions. That's what got us into trouble. It all started Saturday morning with a mysterious message from Sam:

MEET ME IN MY WORKSHOP FOR THE ANSWER TO EVERYTHING. BRING *THE BOOK*.

Fred and I met Sam in his room in the apartment where he lives with his mom. He calls it his workshop. He also calls it his lab, his library, or his control room. It all depends on what he's working on. Fred and I don't ask him why. We just know he's weird.

This time Sam's room—I mean workshop—was covered with posters, drawings, and diagrams. Those giant illustrated books of warplanes and tanks and battleships were stacked everywhere.

"This time I've got it," said Sam. "This time I've really got it."

"Got what?" said Fred. "Bad breath? You've always got that." Fred whacked Sam on the head with his NASCAR hat. Sam was so intense, he didn't even notice. He pointed to a drawing in one of his books.

"Here is the answer to all of our Time Warp problems."

"Really?" I said. "This is the answer to how *The Book* works? Why we can never hang on to it? When it's going to send us time warping?"

"Yes, yes, and yes," said Sam. "All those things."

I looked at the drawing.

"Sam," I said. "This is a drawing of a toilet."

"Good answer," said Fred.

"Not that drawing," said Sam. "I mean the whole book. The whole idea. Look." Sam flipped through *The Book*. "It's a book about inventions. The telephone, the car, flying machines, bubble gum, Velcro, even toilets."

Fred started drawing his own invention—a hot rod. "I call my latest invention The BeastMobile."

"And who would know the most about how these inventions work?" said Sam, still ignoring Fred.

"Uh . . . rocket scientists?" I guessed. "Guys who write encyclopedias?"

"No," said Sam. "The guy who invented the thing."

Fred drew a giant rat driving his invented dragster. "And so a toilet is the answer to all of our time warp problems? I don't get it."

"Forget the toilet," said Sam. "Do I have to explain everything? We find the person who invented *The Book*. That way we find out the answer to how it works."

I took *The Book* out of my backpack. It's a small book really. Blue cover with weird silver designs. Kind of light. You wouldn't think it's as powerful as it is. I put it carefully on the edge of Sam's desk.

"I never thought of that before," I said. "It just might work."

"Of course it will work," said Sam. "Alexander Graham Bell could tell us how the phone works. Thomas Edison could tell us how the lightbulb works. Thomas Crapper could tell us how the toilet works. . . ."

Fred looked up from his drawing. "Are you kidding me?"

"No," said Sam. "The inventor of *The Book*

should be able to tell us anything we want to know about *The Book*."

"I mean, are you kidding about a guy named Crapper?" said Fred. "That can't be for real."

Sam opened one of his books and read, "Thomas Crapper, a London plumber, born in 1836. Though Alexander Cummings is generally credited with inventing the first flush toilet in 1775, Mr. Crapper and his plumbing business most likely gave us his name as a synonym for 'toilet' or 'bathroom.'"

"Too bad for him," said Fred.

I moved *The Book* as far away from Sam's book as possible. "Let's not get *The Book* too close to anything we might be really be sorry for," I said.

Fred pinned his finished drawing on Sam's wall. "I think for once in his life, Sam has got a good idea. But how do we find the inventor of *The Book*?"

"Right here," said Sam. He pointed to a picture of an old guy with long white hair and a long white beard. "Leonardo da Vinci."

Fred and I looked closer at Sam's book. There was the drawing of Leonardo, surrounded by his paintings and other sketches from his notebooks.

"Isn't he the guy who did that Mona Lisa painting?" said Fred.

"Exactly," said Sam. "And he drew all of this other stuff."

Fred held his drawing next to a Leonardo sketch of an ugly bald guy with a huge nose. "Not bad."

"But I don't get it," I said. "Leonardo was an artist. How does that make him the inventor of *The Book*?"

Sam picked up another one of his giant books. "Leonardo was a famous artist. But he was also an amazing scientist and an *inventor*. Did you know he made drawings for a helicopter? And a submarine? And a tank? All way back around 1500. And look at this."

Sam dug through more of his library books. He had that wild look in his eye he gets when he's on to something.

"I've done the research. The man was a genius," said Sam. "He must have been the one who invented *The Book*."

"Sure Sam," said Fred. Fred pointed to his head and twirled his finger around in the universal sign for crazy.

"There," said Sam. He flipped open a book to one of Leonardo's drawings.

"Sam," said Fred. "I'm no genius, and I can draw better than that. It's a naked guy with four arms and four legs."

"No, you moron," said Sam. "It's Leonardo's drawing that solves the problem of turning a square into a circle. And look at Leonardo's backwards writing. I think he used this to hide the secret of time warping."

"I think it shows you've finally cracked," said Fred. "Tell him, Joe."

I couldn't tell him anything because I was standing there with my mouth open.

"Joe?" said Fred.

I stared at the Leonardo drawing. I couldn't move.

Fred helped me the way he always helps. He whacked me on the head with his hat. "Snap out of it."

"That drawing," I said. "I think it's the same one that's on the inside cover of *The Book*. And it has the same backwards writing."

I opened the front cover of *The Book*. There was Leonardo's drawing and the writing.

"I knew it!" said Sam. "Look, right here it says 'Thank You, Time Warp Trio.'"

"Whoa," said Fred. "So Leonardo da Vinci invented *The Book*?"

I saw the first wisp of pale green mist drift out of Leonardo's drawing.

"I guess we'll find out soon enough," I said.

The mist grew thicker and began to circle around Sam's workshop.

Fred suddenly looked panicked. "The mist came out of the da Vinci drawing, right? Cause if it came out of the Thomas Crapper drawing, I will make an invention to give you both a smackdown."

The green time-traveling mist thickened and swirled around and around like . . . well, like . . . a toilet flushing.

I thought I heard a faint roar and a whoosh.

And we swirled down the drain of time.

THREE

"–RE!" yelled Leonardo.

We were goners. No trick could save us now. My life didn't flash before my eyes like they say it does. But I did see a few commercials. I remember thinking it was kind of sad. My last thought was going to be about breakfast cereal.

The guns on Leonardo's wooden tank fired in a quick *pop pop pop*.

Fred, Sam, and I fell together. A sharp pain shot through my chest. Light exploded. Someone laughed.

Someone kept laughing. Someone kept laughing louder and harder. Someone was laughing so hard they could hardly breathe.

I opened one eye to check my wounds. I moved Sam's elbow out of my chest. The sharp pain went away.

The someone laughing was Leonardo. He pointed

at us and bent over laughing. He pointed to the tank and laughed some more.

The guns of the tank waved back and forth. Sticking out of each gun barrel was a wooden rod. Hanging from each rod was a square of cloth. Written on each cloth was the word *Rombo!*

"*Rombo!* Fantastico!" said Leonardo. He wiped the tears from his eyes. "You see the joke? My idea is *Rombo!* The word for the sound the gun would make is written there."

Fred, Sam, and I sat up. Leonardo's men untied us.

"You invented that joke?" said Sam. "That's a classic. I told you guys he was a genius."

I was still having a little trouble breathing. And it wasn't just from Sam's elbow.

"So you weren't really going to shoot us as spies?" I said.

"Goodness no," said Leonardo. "You must know I would never kill anything." He waved a hand at his wooden tank invention. "For this I get paid—to invent machines. But my real work is to discover the world."

Fred checked out the wheels on the tank. "This is a nice ride. I bet you could build a great racing machine."

Leonardo stroked his beard. "Machines for racing? That could be very interesting." He took out a thin blue book and drew a quick sketch in it.

"So *The Book* is really yours?" I said.

"This?" said Leonardo. "Oh yes. I have hundreds of them. They hold the world in them. They move me across the very fabric of time and space."

"No kidding," said Fred.

"Wow," I said. I couldn't believe we had finally met the inventor of *The Book*. "We need to ask you about a million questions."

Leonardo looked at us with that half-smile of his. "And I also have some questions. Like who made your glass lenses? How do your shoes fasten without laces? What is the meaning of the number eight on your hat? What is that on your jerkin?"

Leonardo pointed to a spot on Fred's T-shirt. Fred looked down. Leonardo lifted his finger, flicking Fred's nose and flipping his hat off his head.

Leonardo laughed again. "I just invented that one yesterday."

"Another classic," said Sam.

I still couldn't believe it. We were standing in Italy, five hundred years ago, joking with Leonardo da Vinci—the inventor of *The Book*. Though like Sam said, it did make sense. He invented so many other things. I had a million questions.

"So . . . so . . . how do you fit everything into such a small book? How does it work? Why doesn't everyone know about it?"

Leonardo looked around and lowered his voice. "I do protect many of my secrets with codes and riddles and my backwards writing. Some drawings

I change so the war machines will not really work. What is inside my notebooks is not meant for everyone."

"So true," said Sam, nodding like an expert inventor himself. "We, of course, have figured out mostly how everything works. We just need to know . . . uh . . . exactly how."

Leonardo looked thoughtful. He held up the thin blue book. He started to say, "You see—"

When suddenly, the boom of hoofbeats filled the air. Three, four, five horses and their riders burst around the corner of the road. A small, muscular man with a buzz cut and leather armor jumped off his horse. He stood in front of us with his hands on his hips.

"All right, da Vinci. Where's my dang war machine?"

"Captain Nassti," said Leonardo. "So good to see you. As you can see, we are still testing."

"Don't give me that bullcrap," said Nassti. "I've got a war going on, da Vinci. I don't want excuses. I want results *now*, civilian."

Captain Nassti glared at Leonardo. Captain Nassti glared at the wooden tank. Captain Nassti glared at us. He had to do something. He snatched

the thin blue book out of Leonardo's hand.

"I am confiscating this here book as Official Army Property." Then he pointed to us. "And I am making you three sorry sacks of dog dung Official Army Volunteers."

"Who? Us?" said Sam, looking around behind us for three sorry sacks of dog dung.

"Who? Us?" repeated Captain Nassti in a whiny voice. "No, I mean the three little birdies in the tree. *Yes, you*! you meatheads," screamed Captain Nassti. "Fall in! On the double!"

We looked at Leonardo. He held out his hands in the universal signal that means, "Sorry. Nothing I can do."

Captain Nassti stormed off. He didn't seem like a very nice man. He didn't seem like a very happy man. But he did have *The Book*. And we didn't seem to have much choice.

"Follow me, you maggots," yelled our new leader. "You're in the army now."

FOUR

"Dis id disgustig," said Sam, holding his nose with one hand.

Fred held up his very small brush, just about the size of a toothbrush.

He was not happy. "And the minute we get finished," he said, "I am going to keep my promise and personally smack down both of you."

I scrubbed one of the wooden outhouse toilet seats with my mini brush. "It could be worse," I said. "We could have been thrown into the middle of a battle."

"I'd take my chances with arrows and cannonballs," said Fred, "instead of scrubbing the Italian army's crapper with a toothbrush."

The wooden door to the army outhouse slammed open. It was Captain Nassti.

"What's all the happy chatter in here?" yelled Nassti. "Not enough fireholes to keep you busy?"

"Uh, no," said Sam.

"No *what*?" screamed Nassti. He stuck his face two inches away from Sam's nose.

"I mean yes?" said Sam, leaning back, trying not to fall in the toilet hole.

"Yes *what*, soldier?"

"Yes, we have plenty of—"

"*Nooooo*!" yelled Nassti. His face was turning colors again.

"You say 'Yes, *Sir*!"

"Oh . . . *sir*!" yelled Sam.

"*Yes, SIR*!" we all yelled.

Nassti looked at all three of us. He really looked like he was going to explode. "So you think you're smart guys? Just like your smart-guy boss, da Vinci, huh?"

"Well—" said Sam.

"Shut your piehole, soldier," yelled Nassti. "If I hear so much as one more little peep, bark, or foof out of you, you will be down there where the sun don't shine for the rest of your natural life. DO I MAKE MYSELF CLEAR??!!"

Sam opened his mouth to say yes . . . then wisely decided to just nod his head.

Captain Nassti pulled *The Book* out of his leather

belt. "And I don't know what funny tricks you and your boss think you're pulling. This writing don't make no sense."

He shook *The Book* at our faces. We stood at attention. He was so close to us. I could almost see Fred thinking about just jumping him and grabbing *The Book*.

Nassti lowered his voice to a low growl. "But I am going to figure this out. And when I do, you can grab your sorry hind ends and kiss them goodbye." Nassti whacked *The Book* on the end of the outhouse bench with a *smack*!

Fred, Sam, and I jumped.

Captain Nassti shoved *The Book* back in his belt, and returned his voice to its regular yell. "You earthworms have until sundown to get this crapper spit-shine clean! Then we are going to have a little talk! Understood?"

"*Yes, Sir*!" yelled Fred and I. Sam nodded as loud as he could.

Captain Nassti turned and slammed the door behind him.

The three of us sat down on the tile floor.

"Whoa," said Fred. He pushed his hat back on his head. "That guy is seriously nuts."

"Oh man," said Sam. "We are in deep . . . trouble now. Can you imagine what will happen if he figures out how to use *The Book* to start time warping around? He'll blow up the whole world before we have a chance to be born."

"I knew this was a stupid idea," said Fred, flicking his brush at Sam.

"This part wasn't my idea," said Sam, flicking his brush back at Fred.

"You said you had all of the answers."

"You said it was a good idea."

"You're full of it."

"You're fuller of it."

"So are you."

"I know you are, but what am I?"

Sam and Fred jumped each other and rolled around on the outhouse floor in a double headlock.

"Guys, guys!" I said. "Knock it off. This is not that big of a problem. We've been in a lot worse jams. And this time we have the inventor of *The Book* to help us out."

Sam and Fred quit wrestling.

"That is a good point," said Sam fixing his glasses.

"True," said Fred, fixing his hat. "So what's the plan?"

The afternoon sun shone through the one little window. We didn't have much time. We had to find Leonardo da Vinci in the middle of a strange town in the middle of a strange country in the middle of a strange time five hundred years ago.

"You do have a plan, right?" said Fred.

I had no idea where to start.

I said, "Of course I have a plan. Follow me."

FIVE

I had no plan. I only knew we had to get *The Book* away from Captain Nassti. I motioned with my brush for Sam and Fred to follow me.

We tiptoed to the door and opened it a crack. A covered walkway led from our outbuilding to a kind of small stone castle to the right. A long, low building with a row of windows sat to the left. There was no one in sight. The hot sun hung in the cloudless blue sky. Which way to go?

The voice of Captain Nassti exploded out of the low building on the left. We took off for the tower on the right.

"Where are we going?" whispered Sam. "If Nassti comes back and finds us gone, we are dead meat."

Fred said, "If Nassti comes back and finds us there, we're still dead meat."

We snuck into the shadow against the wall of

the stone tower. I was still trying to think of a plan when we heard voices and footsteps coming closer.

"I hope this is part of your plan," said Fred.

The only way out was an open archway into the tower with stone stairs.

"Of course," I said. "Come on."

We ran up the stone steps. Of course the voices followed us.

"Next floor," I said.

Of course the voices still followed us.

"Definitely the next floor."

The footsteps and voices still followed us. There were no more stairs.

We ran down the hallway. I opened the first wooden door. It was a very plain room. One huge dark wooden table. Four or five chairs. Decorated cloths and drapes hanging on the walls.

"Okay," I said. "The plan is we hide

behind those drapes . . . no wait . . . that never works. They always see your shoes sticking out. Under the table."

We crawled under the table and tried to make ourselves very small. The voices grew louder. The door to the room swung open. I could see four feet.

This was definitely not part of the plan.

"Here?" said a voice.

"Ahh . . . no," said another voice. "The maps are in the next room."

The feet turned and walked out. The door closed.

Sam let out one long breath. Fred and I did too. We hadn't even realized we had stopped breathing.

"Let's get out of here," whispered Sam. "We're not going to find *The Book* or Leonardo here."

"Yeah," said Fred. "Later for Leonardo. I say we take care of this ourselves. We surprise attack Nassti. We grab *The Book*. We jet out of here."

"That was my Plan B," I said. "Let's go."

We crawled out from under the table, then heard the voices sounding like they were right next to us.

"If a man is not loyal, he is a poison to me," said a deep, strong voice.

"And that poison must be removed," said a high voice.

We froze and listened. It was the two guys who had first come into our room. Their voices were coming through the drapes covering the doorway to the next room.

"And my military engineer, Leonardo, has not made much progress."

"That is a problem too," said the thin voice. "It would be a shame if someone else ended up like the governor did—cut in two and left in the town square."

Sam's eyes bugged out. He pointed silently to us, and then toward the door.

Fred and I didn't need any translation. Plan C was to get out of there and warn Leonardo that someone was planning to cut him in two and leave the pieces in the town square.

We tiptoed to the door, eased it open, then ran.

But unfortunately for us, and Leonardo, and Plan C—we ran right into one surprised Captain Nassti.

SIX

I'll leave it to you to imagine all of the nasty names Captain Nassti called us. And you probably don't need me to tell you that he yelled all of these nasty names at top Nassti volume.

This, of course, brought out exactly the two guys we did not want to see—the two guys we had heard talking in the room next door.

"Captain, what in the name of heaven is going on out here?" It was the guy with the strong voice. He looked like a lion, ready to pounce.

"Lord Borgia," said Captain Nassti, "I was coming to report to you, and I found these three bottom-feeding crud suckers sneaking around."

Lord Borgia raised one dark eyebrow. "Oh really?" He looked at the thin-lipped weaselly guy with him. "Step into the chamber."

This did not look good. I had to try a new plan.

"Thanks, Mr. Lord Borgia," I said. "We would

love to come in and talk. But we have a very important meeting where we are supposed to be . . . right now."

"Zip it, numbnertz," said Captain Nassti. "Lord Borgia does not ask. He commands!"

Captain Nassti kicked and shoved and slapped us into the room behind Lord Borgia and his friend.

So much for Plan D.

We stood in front of the two men, who sat down at a table. Maps and diagrams covered the top.

Lord Borgia folded his hands and looked us over. He was one scary looking guy. His long dark hair, mustache, and thin line of beard on his chin made him definitely look like a cat. A big hungry cat. A king of the jungle kind of cat.

No one said anything. Finally Lord Borgia spoke.

"You look too young to be spies. Who do you work for?"

"Such strange clothing," said the thin guy. He checked out our blue jeans and T-shirts. "You must be from Venice."

I looked at his clothes. He wore a long red robe with a long black vest over it. I thought he looked pretty strange himself. But I didn't think that

would be a very good thing to say at the moment.

I couldn't remember if we were on Plan E, F, or G. But I knew we needed a new plan, quick.

"Why does everyone think we're spies?" said Fred. "We're not spies. We're three guys from Brooklyn."

"Yeah," said Sam. "We're three guys just looking for . . . well not really looking for anything, because that's what spies do and you know we're not spies because . . ."

Lord Borgia and his friend did not look like they were believing a word of any of this. I glanced at the maps and drawings on the table in front of them. And that's when it hit me—Plan F (or maybe G or H).

" . . . because we are inventors," I said. "We have been called in, from a very long way away, to help Leonardo da Vinci."

"Oh?" said Lord Borgia.

"Yes," I said. "We're here to help Leonardo finish up a most top secret invention he is working on for you. With our invention, you will be unstoppable."

"That's a load of donkey squat," said Captain Nassti.

Lord Borgia held up one hand. "That will be for me to decide, Captain. Tell us more."

"Well I wish I could," I said. "But it is very top secret."

Sam and Fred nodded.

Sam pretended to zip his lip, then made a face at Captain Nassti. Sam turned back. Nassti smacked him on the back of the head.

"That's enough, Captain," said Lord Borgia. "Leonardo and his assistants should have their chance to prove their worth."

Sam turned and made another face at Captain Nassti. Nassti raised his hand to smack Sam again. I saw *The Book* still tucked in his belt.

That's when I thought of a perfect trick and my most brilliant plan. A plan big enough and good enough to solve all of our problems and be Plan X, Y, and Z.

The thin guy spoke. "But surely you can tell Lord Borgia a little something of the idea."

"No can do," said Fred.

"Top-o secret-o," said Sam.

"Of course we can," I said, shaking my head at Sam and Fred. "Where we come from, we have drawn many plans for military machines. We have plans for machines that fly through the air, machines that can dive underwater, machines that bullets . . . or cannonballs . . . just bounce off of. Fred, show Lord Borgia our flying machine invention."

Fred found a blank paper on the table. He drew a nice F-111 attack jet, with a nose cannon and underwing surface-to-air missiles.

"We call it a jet," I said.

"I call it the Hellcat FredJet," said Fred.

Borgia and his friend looked impressed. Sam caught on to the idea, and went with it.

"We've also got some great ideas for aircraft carriers and tanks and this thing I call the computer," said Sam.

"Right," I said. "But our most amazing invention is our Power Drain."

"Right," said Sam. "Our . . . what?"

"Our Power Drain," I said. "Small enough to be used by one finger. I actually have just enough Power Drain with me to give a small demonstration."

"You do?" said Fred.

"I do," I said.

Fred and Sam looked completely confused.

I sprung my plan.

"I will demonstrate our Power Drain on Captain Nassti. If it works, you take us to Leonardo, and you give us that."

I pointed to the the thin blue object stuck in Captain Nassti's belt.

I pointed to *The Book*.

SEVEN

Captain Nassti sat in a chair facing me. *The Book* sat on the table in front of Lord Borgia. It was then I realized that I had never really practiced this trick.

I thought about making a dive for *The Book* and just time warping out of there.

"Well?" said Lord Borgia. He folded his hands over *The Book*. "What is this Power Drain?"

That took care of making a dive for *The Book*. It was trick . . . or die.

"Okay," I said. "But if we show you, we get *The Book* and we get to see Leonardo, right?"

"And if it don't work," said Captain Nassti, "You maggots are mine for the next five years."

I tried not to think of that.

"We have many inventions," I began. "We've shown you our jet, our tank, and our dragster."

Fred held up his drawings.

"But now I will show you just a tiny bit of our

newest, most fearsome invention ever—the Power Drain."

I walked over in front of Captain Nassti and stood with the tips of my shoes almost touching the tips of his boots.

"Captain Nassti," I said. "You are strong, yes?"

"Strong enough to snap your pencil neck, twerp."

I tried to laugh, but it came out more like a choke.

"Right," I said. "So what if I told you we had an invention that could drain away all your power with just one finger?"

"I'd say you been sitting on your brains," said Nassti.

"An invention like that could be very useful," said Lord Borgia's friend.

"Watch closely," I said. I turned to Lord Borgia and his pal. "I am going to use just my one finger to drain Captain Nassti's power. If I turned it up all of the way, you could stop a whole army, of course."

"In your dreams, dog-breath," barked Nassti.

Fred and Sam looked at me like I had lost my mind.

"Sit back," I told Nassti. "Fold your arms across your chest." I pretended to adjust my finger. "I will now drain your power and, with only this one finger on your forehead, hold you in your chair."

I swallowed hard. I pressed my finger against Nassti's forehead. Lord Borgia and his friend leaned forward to watch.

"Power . . . DRAIN! Try to stand up."

Nassti went to stand up.

He couldn't.

"Just a dang minute," he said.

"Stand up, Captain Nassti," said Lord Borgia.

Nassti grunted and tried again. I held him with my one finger. He couldn't stand.

Sam and Fred both yelled, "Yeah!"

To stand up from a sitting position, you need to move your feet forward, throw your head forward, or pull yourself forward with your arms to get you started. My feet in front of Captain Nassti's feet and his arms folded across his chest left him with only the strength of his neck to push against the force of all of me behind my finger.

Nassti puffed. He yelled something really nasty. I decided I'd better not risk holding him much longer.

"I will now remove the Power Drain," I said. I lowered my finger and jumped back.

Captain Nassti exploded out of his chair. "Why, you little rat! Hand-to-hand combat. Right here! Right now!" He got in a crouch, ready to attack.

"Amazing," said Lord Borgia.

"Very impressive," said his pal. "How does it work?"

I got behind one of the chairs with Fred and

Sam. Captain Nassti looked mad enough to tear all three of us to pieces right there.

"We . . . uh . . . are still working on the full invention with Leonardo," I said. "We'll tell you all about it just as soon as we finish. So now we get *The Book* and we'll be heading off to see Leonardo, right?"

"This invention is exactly what I need to defeat the town of Urbo," said Lord Borgia. "In fact—I could rule every town and city." He pulled his beard and squinted his eyes. "That will be all, Captain Nassti. You may go."

Captain Nassti gave us one killer look and stormed out. He didn't really like us before. Now we had a serious enemy.

Lord Borgia held *The Book*. "Your invention will give me my own empire!"

"Absolutely," said Sam.

"Great idea," said Fred.

"Have it ready for me by tomorrow," said Lord Borgia.

"What?" I said. "Oh no, I mean we still have a lot of work to do."

"Lord Borgia does not ask. He commands," said the weaselly guy.

Fred grabbed *The Book* out of Lord Borgia's hand. "Yeah we heard that already," said Fred. "But we are out of here."

Fred held up *The Book* and said, "Eat our time warp dust."

EIGHT

I was thinking it was a shame we never got a chance to ask Leonardo da Vinci how *The Book* really works.

I got ready for the weird roller-coaster time-warping feeling.

But it seemed like we were still standing in the room with Lord Borgia and his friend five hundred years ago.

That's because we were still standing in the room with Lord Borgia and his friend five hundred years ago.

Fred shook *The Book*. "I said—Eat our time warp dust."

Nothing.

Sam grabbed *The Book*. "Let me work the thing." He flipped open the front cover to Leonardo's drawing. "Oh no," he said.

"Oh no what?" I said.

"Oh no, this isn't *The Book*. It really is just one of Leonardo's notebooks."

Lord Borgia looked at the three of us with the look of a cat watching a mouse. He didn't seem to know exactly what we were talking about. And he didn't really seem to care.

"Tomorrow," said Lord Borgia's friend. "Or else maybe you would like some help from Captain Nassti."

"Oh no," said Sam. "Not that."

I took *The Book*. It was full of Leonardo's backwards writing, diagrams, and sketches. It wasn't going to time warp us anywhere. But we didn't have much choice.

"Okay," I said. "We'll think of something. . . . I mean we'll have our invention ready by tomorrow."

Two soldiers appeared. They led us out of the room.

"Splendid," said Lord Borgia. "Please give my best wishes to Leonardo."

NINE

Fred, Sam, and I followed the soldiers through the narrow winding streets of the small Italian town. The sun hung low in the sky.

White stone buildings rose up on both sides of the street. An old lady dressed all in black watched us from a window. Little kids in long tunics ran in and out of the street. No one seemed to really notice us.

"I can't believe you got me into this," said Fred. "All for what? To find out how *The Book* works? We should have gone somewhere to find treasure or build race cars . . ."

We walked by a sidewalk vegetable market.

" . . . or at least somewhere with lots of food."

"But just think," said Sam. "We are going to hang out with Leonardo da Vinci. Maybe he's got *The Book* somewhere else. I'm sure he'll figure something out. The guy is a genius."

"He'd better be," said Fred. "Or else we're all

going to end up being geniuses—at scrubbing toilets."

The soldiers led us down a side alley with a bunch of arched doorways open to the street.

Leonardo da Vinci stepped out of the middle doorway.

"Joe, Sam, Fred da Brooklyn." He held out both arms. "I heard you were coming, so I prepared a little feast."

Leonardo waved off the soldiers, then led us into his workshop. The place was covered in drawings, a painting of a dragon on a shield, clay sculptures of horses, diagrams of gears and pumps and crossbows, brushes and papers and paints.

"Wow," said Sam.

A table off to one side was filled with dishes of olives, plates of cheese, bowls of curly pasta, bread, ham, salami, fruit, and cakes.

"I don't eat meat myself," said Leonardo. "But I thought that you might enjoy the local specialties."

"Now, *that* is genius," said Fred.

We gave Leonardo back his blue notebook. Then we dove right into stuffing ourselves full.

Leonardo wanted to know everything—from

how Velcro worked . . . to the meaning of the number on Fred's hat . . . to who made Sam's glasses . . . to how my finger on the forehead trick worked. He was the most curious guy I have ever met.

In between bites of cheese and bread and ham we told him everything.

"And Lord Borgia and his friend were talking about cutting someone in two and leaving him in the town square," said Sam.

"And we drew him pictures of jets and tanks and helicopters," said Fred.

"And we have to have some kind of fantastic invention by tomorrow," I said. "Or else."

Leonardo munched thoughtfully on a piece of cheese. "Hmmm," he said. "This is serious. Lord Borgia is a man who gets what he wants. He is very powerful. And his friend you met is Niccolò Machiavelli. He is brilliant, and possibly even more dangerous."

"So you must have a plan, right?" said Sam.

Leonardo ate a grape. He thought for a few seconds. "No, not really. How about you?"

Fred stacked ham and cheese and lettuce and olives on a slice of bread. "How about a thin blue book sort of like yours? But one that leaks green mist and warps a person through time and space? You got anything like that?"

Leonardo gave Fred a strange look. "Interesting that you should say that."

"Really?" I said. "Do you have *The Book*?"

"Did you invent *The Book*?" asked Sam.

"I was going to say I've been working on the nature of time and space and the human shape," said Leonardo. He pulled out a piece of paper with a drawing. It was our four-armed guy.

TEN

"That's it!" said Sam.

"So in Brooklyn you also understand the shapes and powers of the human body?" said Leonardo.

"Well, sort of," said Sam.

"Maybe you can help me finish," said Leonardo.

"Right," said Sam. "How does it go again?"

Leonardo traced over his drawing with one finger as he spoke. "The length of a man's outstretched arms is equal to his height. That makes a square."

I nodded.

Fred chomped on his sandwich.

"Raise your arms until your middle fingers are level with the top of your head. The ends of your hands and feet now mark a circle. And so—"

"And so the human body squares the circle," said Sam. "And when you square the circle you open a wormhole in the folded fabric of space/time

. . . which then allows you to time warp anywhere! Right?"

"Hmmm," said Leonardo. "No. I was going to say: And so the center of the circle is your belly button."

"But how does *The Book* take you through time and space?" I said. "Didn't you invent it?"

Leonardo shook his head. "A book that takes you through time and space? I wish I could invent something that amazing. No, I need to find the one missing shape in this problem. Circle. Square. What?"

"So you didn't invent *The Book*?" said Sam. Sam looked like he was going to cry.

Fred looked more closely at the drawing. "Hey, this isn't the same drawing as the one in *The Book*. This guy's only got two legs."

So Leonardo wasn't the inventor of *The Book*. That was bad enough. But the thought of being stuck with Captain Nassti for five years of toilet cleaning made me feel even worse than Sam looked.

"Well," said Fred. "Why am I not surprised? That would have been too easy." He finished off half of his giant sandwich, then said with his mouth full, "We'd better get to work. Got to figure out something to show Borgia tomorrow. Don't need to be toilet scrubbers for life."

It was just like Fred to not worry about what might happen. He just went to work to solve the problem.

"Not the inventor," said Sam in a daze.

And it was just like Sam to come a bit unglued when what he thought was the answer turned out to be not the answer.

The last of the setting sun lit Leonardo's workshop in a warm orange light. We could hear the kids playing in the street. They sounded like they were having fun. But how much fun would it be to be stuck five hundred years ago in Italy? People died of all kinds of Black Plague and things. And I'm pretty sure no one was going to get cable TV for a long, long time.

"I do have several secret inventions I have been working on," said Leonardo. He took down another notebook from a shelf of books. He flipped through the pages. "A cart than runs without horses? A machine to fly through the air? A boat that runs under water?"

"A car, a helicopter, and a submarine," I said. "Those are all great inventions."

"But I would hate to see them end up in the hands of men like Captain Nassti," said Leonardo.

Fred pushed his hat back on his head. "Well, we can't build a car or a submarine or a helicopter by tomorrow anyway. How about something simple to start with?" Fred sketched a bicycle on a page of the notebook.

"Leonardo not inventor of *Book,*" said Sam. He was getting worse, sounding like a caveman.

I thought maybe a trick might cheer him up. "How about this?" I held my nose with both hands like I was praying. "I'll crack my nose." I flicked my thumbnail off my front tooth with a *crack*, while pretending to move my nose.

"That's terrible," said Sam. But he did crack half a smile.

"That's totally stupid," said Fred.

"How do you do that?" said Leonardo.

I showed him the trick. He laughed.

"If I had a plastic cup, I could show you an even better neck-cracking trick," I said. I reached for a breadstick to use for that trick. I knocked over a glass of water.

The water streamed down the table. It was headed for Fred's sandwich. Fred grabbed a long thin wedge of cheese and blocked the stream of water. The water dripped over the edge of the table. Fred's sandwich was saved.

Leonardo stared at Fred's cheese dam. He looked at a map on the wall behind us. He gave a laugh and started practicing cracking his nose.

"What's so funny?" said Fred. "He almost soaked my masterpiece."

"Yes," said Leonardo. "But now we have a plan."

ELEVEN

Leonardo explained his plan. It was simple, powerful, and easy to build.

We put it together using wood and tools from the workshop. That night we slept on straw mattresses in the back of the shop, plenty tired from a long day of scrubbing toilets and building inventions.

Leonardo made all of the arrangements to show our new invention to Lord Borgia and his friend Machiavelli.

We met them outside of town, right near a stream and the woods where we had time warped in.

Sam and I stood next to Leonardo. Fred was at his post with our invention next to the stream.

"Okay," said Leonardo. "Everything ready?"

Fred checked under the tarp. "Ready."

I fixed a dry stick under one arm. "Ready."

Sam rolled his head around, stretching his neck. "Ready."

Leonardo pointed to the front of Sam's shirt. "But what is the meaning of that?"

Sam looked down.

Leonardo flicked Sam's nose, then laughed like a maniac.

Just then we heard the sound of horses galloping toward us. The horses and riders thundered around the corner of the road. Lord Borgia and Machiavelli got off their horses. They were followed by an unexpected third rider—Captain Nassti.

"Oh, crap," said Sam.

"What did you just say, soldier?" yelled Captain Nassti.

"Snap, snap," said Sam, backing away from Nassti.

Leonardo took over. "Welcome, noble gentlemen . . . and you too, Captain. My fellow inventors—"

Leonardo swept his hand to include Fred, Sam, and me.

"—and I are ready to show you our most amazing invention."

"This had better be good," said Nassti, "Or your butts belong to the army."

Leonardo nodded. He was definitely right about not letting guys like Nassti see his inventions.

"Please," said Lord Borgia. "I have the greatest faith in Leonardo. That's why I made him my military engineer."

"Thank you, Lord Borgia," said Leonardo. "Now step closer and observe."

The three men stepped closer.

"The challenge is—how to take the town of Urbo," said Leonardo.

"Smash them. Pound them. Then smash them again with everything we've got," said Nassti. He smacked one beefy fist into his other palm.

"Well, yes, you could do that," said Leonardo. "But my assistants and I have learned how to use a much smaller force to big effect. Like this."

Leonardo held his hands up and gave his nose a good fake *crack*.

"Or like this." Leonardo waved to me and Sam.

I grabbed Sam's head with two hands, then gave it a twist while I secretly snapped the stick under my arm with another loud *crack*.

Borgia and Machiavelli looked puzzled. Captain Nassti looked completely confused.

"Yes," said Lord Borgia. "But your three assistants promised me they would have their Power Drain weapon ready. How are these stunts going to help us take the town?"

"Yeah," said Nassti. "You going to crack everybody's nose and neck?"

"Not at all," said Leonardo calmly. "Our demonstration shows how we use the smallest force for the greatest action." Leonardo pointed to the small stream. "Urbo is a town on a river. It depends on the river to move its trade. It depends on the river for food and water. It depends on the river for its life. Correct?"

Borgia and Machiavelli nodded.

Nassti just looked confused.

"So instead of wasting your money and the lives of men and horses in a costly battle, we apply just a little force with the proper invention. The town is yours," said Leonardo. "Fred?"

Fred threw back the tarp and showed our invention—three planks of wood fastened together and hinged at one end on the bank of the stream.

Leonardo gave the signal, and Fred flipped our wooden dam up and over, across the width of the stream.

The little stream pushed against our wooden dam and changed direction to flow down into a meadow. It worked just like Fred's cheese dam. Below the boards, the stream dried quickly to a small trickle.

"Our simple invention diverts the river. Urbo is without water. Urbo surrenders. Urbo is yours."

"Hmmm," said Lord Borgia. He tugged his little beard.

"Very simple," said Machiavelli.

"That ain't right," said Nassti. "Where's all the guns and explosions and men and horses and cannons?"

The morning sun suddenly seemed very hot. A single bird chirped.

It was do or die. If Lord Borgia didn't like this plan, we were sunk. Leonardo would never be the genius he was supposed to be. We would never see home again. We would be slaves of Captain Nassti five hundred years ago.

"No cannons," said Lord Borgia.

"No men or horses in battle," said Machiavelli.

"Terrible," said Nassti. "A disgrace to our army."

I thought we were sunk.

Then Lord Borgia said one word. "Genius."

"Brilliant," said Machiavelli.

"Sissies," said Captain Nassti. He stomped off, jumped on his horse, and rode off in a cloud of dust.

We were saved. Leonardo could go on being a genius. The Time Warp Trio could go on . . . well . . . we could just go on . . . without having to clean toilets for the rest of our lives.

And right at that moment, it felt like genius.

TWELVE

So we were saved by Fred da Brooklyn's invention and Leonardo da Vinci's plan.

Lord Borgia loved the idea so much he gave "most excellent and dearly beloved Leonardo and his assistants" a free pass to travel anywhere in the country.

"And listen to this," said Leonardo, reading from the official paper. "Give him any aid, assistance, and favor he asks for. Let no man act otherwise unless you wish to feel my anger. Lord Borgia."

Fred, Sam, and I sat around the table in Leonardo's studio. We were celebrating with another feast. Fred's idea.

"I knew you were a genius," Sam said to Leonardo. "Even if you didn't invent *The Book*. Didn't I tell you guys?"

"That was a nice piece of work," said Fred.

"I liked the way you figured out how to use both

the nose crack and the neck crack tricks," I said. "You should invent those clear plastic cups. They make the best cracking noises."

We ate chicken and more cheese and bread and pasta. It was a little scary to think that we were going to be stuck somewhere in Italy, somewhere in the 1500s. But at least we were going to be hanging out with Leonardo da Vinci and getting plenty to eat.

"Thanks to you three," said Leonardo, "my inventions are safe."

"And now you'll be able to paint your most famous painting—the *Mona Lisa*—instead of cleaning toilets," said Sam.

Leonardo gave Sam a puzzled look. It's hard to explain to people about knowing the future.

Fred worked on another one of his food creations. "Except this is going to be a real problem if we don't invent cable TV, video games, and the skateboard real soon. We'd better get started."

"I do believe I could sketch out the basic idea of broadcast television and maybe a simple computing device," said Sam. "I'm sure Leonardo could take it from there."

Leonardo stared at his drawing of the man in the square and the circle.

"Okay," said Fred. "So here is the first step toward modern civilization." He showed us a triangular piece of flatbread layered with cheese and slices of salami.

"What is that?" asked Leonardo.

"The pepperoni pizza slice," said Fred.

Sam looked up from sketching his diagram of a computer. "Oh, and by the way, that's the shape missing from your drawing—the triangle."

"What?" said Leonardo. He looked from Fred's pizza slice to his drawing.

"The triangle," said Sam. He pushed his glasses up on his nose. "Draw the guy's legs spread out. His legs make two sides of your third shape—the

isosceles triangle. Square. Circle. Triangle.”

Leonardo looked at his drawing.

Leonardo looked at Fred’s pizza slice.

His eyes lit up. “Yes! That’s it!”

Leonardo pulled another one of his notebooks from the shelf. He flipped open the front cover. There was another copy of his man inside the square and circle. Leonardo drew two more legs on the guy just as Sam had described them. He looked at the finished drawing. He looked at us.

“Fantastico,” said Leonardo. He held Sam by the shoulders. “Sam da Brooklyn—genius. Thank you.”

Leonardo da Vinci wrote across the top of the drawing in the notebook. He handed *The Book* to Sam.

Sam read the writing. “‘ oirT qraW emiT ,uoy knahT.’”

I thought I saw a small line of pale green mist snake around Sam’s hands.

Leonardo traced the square, the circle, then the triangle with one finger.

"Oh wait," said Sam. "That's your backwards writing. 'Thank you, Time Warp Trio.'"

Leonardo closed the cover of *The Book* in Sam's hands. It was a dark blue cover with twisting silver designs.

"It's *The Book*," said Fred.

And it was.

Now I definitely saw the thickening green mist swirl around Sam and Leonardo.

"What? How? Who?" said Sam.

"Arrivederci," said Leonardo da Vinci. He sat back in his chair and smiled that half smile of his that looked so familiar.

The green time warping mist swirled around us, and we were gone like the smile on the Mona Lisa.

THIRTEEN

I know I've never done a very good job of describing what it's like to time warp. It's not that it's a big secret. It's just that it's kind of impossible to describe.

I mean imagine trying to describe to somebody who can't taste what chocolate ice cream tastes like. There's a lot of stuff going on. But you don't even have the words to start.

Though after this adventure, I might say time warping is a lot like a high-speed, full-body toilet flush, and leave it at that.

So we high-speed, full-body flushed back to the exact same time and place we had left—Saturday morning in Sam's workshop.

Sam fixed his glasses.

Fred pulled his hat.

I grabbed *The Book* out of Sam's hands and shoved it deep into my backpack.

"Unbelievable," said Sam. "I think we just met the one guy who understands how *The Book* works. And he called me a genius."

I closed Sam's book about Thomas Crapper and moved it away from my backpack just to be safe.

Sam flipped open his Leonardo da Vinci book.

"Check it out," said Sam. "There's the Mona Lisa, his self portrait when he's older, drawings of his tank, his helicopter—"

"And there's my bicycle sketch," said Fred.

And there it was. I read, "Leonardo's sketch of a primitive bicycle."

"Who are they calling primitive?" said Fred. "Now that's a real work of genius."

"Look, look," said Sam. He was actually jumping up and down. "Here's the time warping sketch of that four-armed guy . . . with my extra legs triangle!"

"Let's remember that triangle idea came from my pizza slice invention," said Fred.

Sam didn't hear a word Fred said.

He had the same wild look in his eye that Leonardo had when he was in his workshop.

“We’ve got to go back and talk to Leonardo,” said Sam. “Trace the shapes in *The Book* and let’s go.”

“I don’t know,” I said. I was still feeling a little time-warp flushed. I didn’t really feel like getting flushed again. And I most definitely didn’t feel like running into Captain Nassti ever again.

“I really think,” I said, “the best thing to do now would be to—Oh no! What is that?!” I yelled.

I pointed to Sam’s shirt.

He looked.

And you know I got him.

I got him good.

Genius.

Inventors' Workshop

Leonardo da Vinci was an amazing artist, scientist, engineer, and inventor. But who's got time for all of that, right?

So let's just start by each inventing one thing to make this world a better place. Okay?

Here are our inventions:

FRED
Pepperoni pizza slice blueprint

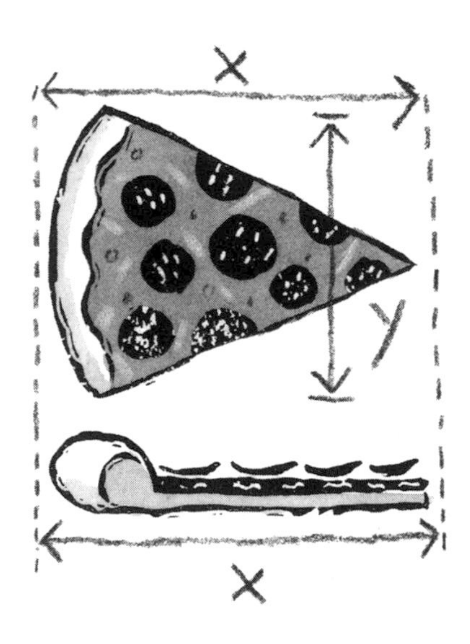

JOE

Diagram of cracking-plastic-cup-under-arm trick

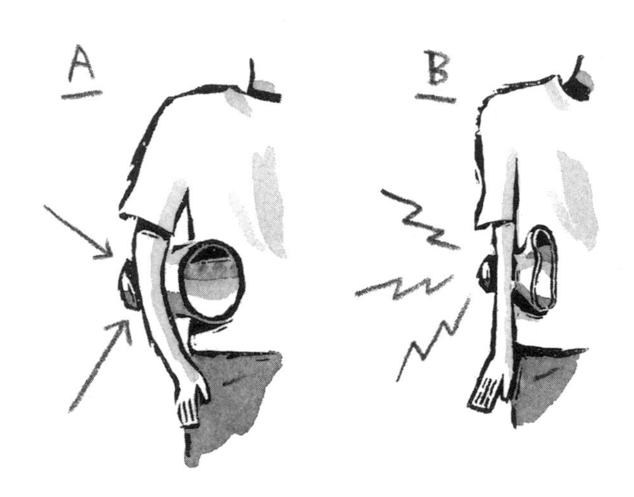

SAM

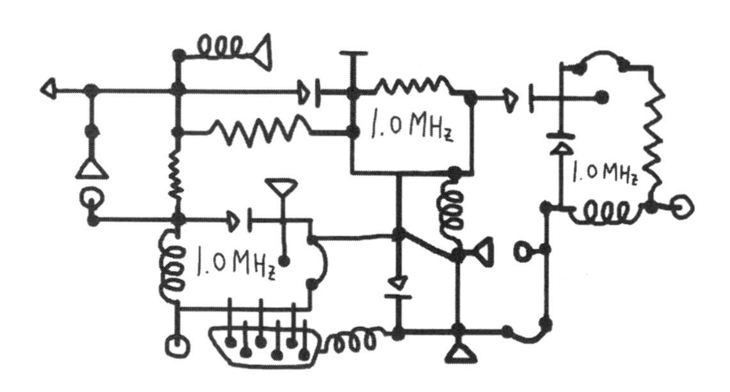